Robbed

LK WOLLETT

Published by LK WOLLETT, 2023.

ROBBED

First edition. November 18, 2023.

ISBN: 979-8223809586

Written by LK WOLLETT.

Robbed

Chapter 1

Though they were born 'identical twins', nothing could be further from reality. First of all, their mother, Katie, wasn't organized enough to have two sets of anything matching, and second, the younger of the two, Shawna, didn't want to be a twin. It wasn't something she decided in her head; it was more like something in her composition that demanded independence. Being a twin or not being a twin was no issue to Myrna who kept herself busy with the task at hand whether it was playing with dolls as a child, doing homework as a student, or getting a job after college graduation.

Though their IQ was the same, Shawna's lack of interest in studies was recognized early and, counselors suggested to Katie and her husband, Randy, that Shawna would have higher grades and a higher probability of graduating if they enrolled her in classes like art, bookkeeping, or home management. This put the twins in completely different social circles. Shawna's friends pushed against boundaries and prohibitions resulting in drunken parties and free sex while Myrna was home in the evenings. Though Katie and Randy wanted Shawna to be home with them, they weren't strong enough to fight with her night after night. When Myrna met Kevin, who she wanted to spend time with, their 'dates' were spent with parents or at church events because Kevin was a devout Christian. As Myrna heard Christian scripture, her faith grew to the point that she decided to follow Jesus[1]. Knowing that Jesus wanted her to have sex with her husband and no-one else, she planned to remain a virgin[2] until she got married.

The night before Myrna left for college, Katie and Randy invited relatives and neighbors to a cook-out. Shawna, joining Myrna who was seated at a picnic table, was excited for Myrna thinking that Myrna was finally free.

"You can par-tay now, Girl," Shawna exclaimed.

"Not sure I want to 'par-tay'," Myrna answered seriously.

"Have you ever had a beer?" Shawna taunted. "Don't knock it 'til you try it."

"I've tasted it," Myrna admitted, "but I'm not interested. I've seen you drunk and out of control, Shawna. I don't want to be like that. Plus it's not good for you."

"Is that because of Je-Sus?" Shawna sneered, wagging her head.

"Jesus wasn't against alcohol[3]," Myrna responded. "He was against being drunk."

"I suppose you're a virgin, too," Shawna mocked, rolling her eyes.

"I am and I will be on my wedding night," Myrna replied firmly.

One of Shawna's friends, Troy, was talking to her dad, Randy.

"Look at Troy talking to Dad," Shawna giggled. "I think he wants to sleep with me. See that bulge in his jeans? How can you resist a hunk like that?"

"I hope he wants more than sex from you," Myrna said with concern.

"What else is there?" Shawna blurted with a laugh.

"A relationship, a home and family," Myrna offered. "You can't party your entire life. Mom and Dad make it look easy but they work hard to provide this home for us."

"You're such a downer!" Shawna exclaimed and walked over to Troy.

"I'll pray for you," Myrna whispered.

College for Myrna was a series of tasks that she focused on and completed. Though her roommates pressured her to party, she found a church where she could mingle with other students and townspeople her age. She also kept in touch with Kevin who visited occasionally.

Shawna chose to work at a gas station where she became popular with the regular customers. One of the customers was a semi-truck driver with an impressive bulge who came through every week. His cab was a deep purple with streaks of gold lightening. Taller than most men, probably with help of cowboy boots, he always wore some form of plaid shirt over a tee shirt and cowboy hat. He called her "Girlie" in a deep, Western drawl, and asked her when she was going away with him, promising her nights under the stars; somehow this was all very appealing to Shawna. One day, he got his usual drinks, snacks and smokes, put some cash on the counter and a little black box.

"What's this?" Shawna asked, staring at him with wonder.

"Why don't you open it and see," answered the cowboy glibly.

"A ring?" Shawna marveled, looking up at him with question.

"Yes! A ring, damit!" the cowboy blurted. "Don't you know when you're getting proposed to? Put it on!"

"Oh, wow!" Shawna exclaimed as the line of customers got longer.

"Well?" the cowboy asked as he picked up his purchases.

"Well," Shawna hesitated, looking into his begging eyes, then she blurted. "Yes!"

"Let's go then," the cowboy commanded as he walked out the door.

Shawna ran from behind the counter and followed the cowboy abandoning customers to leave money or walk out without paying. The cowboy, Rick, pulled his truck into a parking lot and pulled Shawna close to him, caressing her lips and breasts. In moments he had her stripped and pulled into the back of the cab, revealing his bulge. He trembled visibly as he eased it inside her and focused on every thrust.

"From the first time I saw you," he whispered, "I wanted to feel myself inside you."

When he withdrew, he pulled on his pants and moved to the front seat.

Without looking back at her, he stated, "We have to get going."

"I need my clothes," Shawna said, checking her hair in a mirror. "I need to tell my parents."

The big semi pulled in front of Shawna's house but no-one was home. After packing a bag, Shawna sat on her bed and wrote a note explaining that she was eloping and she would call. Then she climbed into the purple cab and rode west with the cowboy.

As they were driving, a Western love song was playing but Rick wasn't talkative. If Shawna had a question, he answered it but he never sought information from her. After eight hours of driving, Rick pulled into a truck stop for gas and food. They ate at a picnic table then pulled into an overnight parking area. Again, Rick stripped Shawna, penetrated her and fondled her vagina. She fell asleep but woke briefly every time Rick penetrated her.

The next morning, Shawna asked about bathing and Rick said he would deliver his load today then he would take her to his house. As it was getting dark, they arrived at an old farm house Rick inherited from his parents, in need of maintenance but livable. Because Rick had been gone a week, the yard needed mowed. Both were hungry so they ate in the small kitchen then he took her to his bedroom. He ran a bath and they washed each other, with some laughs and giggles. He then carried her into the bedroom for his usual routine. She fell asleep to be awaken briefly by penetrations.

In the morning, the lawn mower woke Shawna and she went to the kitchen for coffee and breakfast, though the cupboards and fridge were practically empty. Finding a vacuum, she cleaned the rooms downstairs and mopped the kitchen and downstairs bathroom. When the mower stopped, she looked outside and Rick had the hood of the truck open. So she took the vacuum upstairs to clean. When that was done, she walked outside to Rick who was black with grease. When he tried to embrace her, she ran from him, laughing, demanding that he wash first. Returning to the house, she was hungry so she nibbled on some snack food but she wanted to go to the grocery so she could cook and bake. Gathering sheets, pillow cases and clothes that needed washed, she started the washing machine. While watching a movie and folding the laundry, she was glad to hear Rick come into the house. As he came toward her, she got up giggling and backed away from his greasy hands. This time he caught her and took her into the bathroom for another bath and penetration. Rather than falling asleep, she told him she was hungry so he suggested pizza and he ordered delivery. When the pizza arrived, Rick wanted Shawna to stay nude so they ate on the bed. When Shawna mentioned going to the grocery, Rick said they had a load tomorrow and would eat on the road. After they were done with pizza, true to his word, Rick took blankets to the back yard with a nude Shawna and fondled her under the stars, with penetrations throughout the night. Shawna agreed now with Myrna that there is more to life than sex. As she studied the ring Rick had given her, she was relieved he never made their union legal.

In a few months, Myrna posted that she had accepted Kevin's proposal. When the wedding date was finalized, Myrna asked Shawna to be the maid of honor. When Shawna told Rick that she needed to be home for Shawna's wedding, he acknowledged; then he dropped her off at her parents and picked her up when the wedding was over. Shortly after, Myrna posted pictures of the house she and Kevin were building. By this time, Shawna knew that Rick would never leave his parents' house nor would he spend money to improve it. Though Rick always had money, Shawna had no idea how much or where he kept it. Because Shawna explained that she needed fruits and vegetables to keep her figure, he finally took her to the grocery, otherwise, if she needed something they could not buy at a truck stop or grocery store, he would pick it up or order it for her. He stated often that she didn't need clothes; that he liked to see her nude but when she would not comply, he bought her bras, panties and cowboy boots.

Boredom was Shawna's biggest problem. In the truck, Rick didn't talk and the routes they took were always the same. Having the cell phone was some diversion and would occupy her a few hours. At the farm house, she spent time cleaning; she searched for recipes to cook or bake; she planted a garden; she took walks; she responded to Rick's advances; and the rest of the time she read free e-books or watched TV. Anything else would take money. She thought about not going with

Rick on his route or getting a job but it seemed obvious to her that he expected her to ride with him, and she felt uneasy giving another woman a chance with him.

One morning, Shawna woke feeling sick with a rash on her stomach. When Rick saw it, he drove her to a hospital, and they were told it was shingles. When they got home, Rick did not make his usual advances and when he left on his route, he didn't take Shawna. A week later, when Rick returned, he checked her stomach and, when he saw the rash was gone, he took her upstairs for a bath and some penetrations. On the next road trip, after dinner at a picnic table, when Rick and Shawna climbed into the back of the cab, Shawna spotted a pair of panties on the floor. Holding them in front of Rick's eyes, Shawna asked where they came from.

"Nobody special," Rick answered flatly, looking out the window.

"But somebody," Shawna pressed.

"It doesn't matter," Rick insisted firmly. "She's not like you. She's just temporary."

"You're saying you love my vagina more than hers?" Shawna quipped.

"Yeah, you could say that," Rick replied with a smile and a nod. "You were sick for a long time. You expect me to wait?"

"Yeah, you could say that," Shawna replied with a frown and a nod.

Shawna moved to the front seat hoping that Rick would leave her alone but pretty sure he wouldn't. She felt she had endured with patience, these last few years, Rick's lifestyle and sexual preferences, and this betrayal gave her permission to leave him. Now she needed the courage to say the words. After Rick pulled her to the back of the truck and penetrated her, Shawna announced that she didn't want to ride with him anymore. He nodded solemnly. The next day, he dropped her off at her parents' house but not before he penetrated her one last time and asking her, with begging eyes, if she really wanted to leave. Though she felt sorry for him, she pulled herself away and laid his ring on the passenger seat.

Chapter 2

Myrna had a baby girl, Rachael, and, because Kevin's job as a computer system manager was paying well, Myrna was able to stay home with the baby. Shawna got a job at a discount store and soon joined a group who like to party. Occasionally she would click with a guy and spend the night with him but a relationship never formed. After a couple of years, though, Shawna stopped partying, feeling empty, and took advantage of career improvement courses offered by the discount store. In another couple of years, Shawna was promoted to assistant manager and her income allowed her to move in with a friend from the store, Maggie, who had two children, Jim, age ten, and Phyllis, age eight. Maggie kept Jim busy with sports and they all went to his games.

In the bleachers, one sunny afternoon, Shawna started bantering with a guy sitting close by, Jack, who had the muscles and build of a football linebacker. When the game was over, Jack invited Shawna to dinner where they kept each other laughing the entire night. He was a football scout who travelled the state watching the upcoming crop of football players. She accepted his invitation to his hotel room and enjoyed every minute as he prepared her for a bath, removing her shirt and bra, taking time to stroke and mouth her well-defined breasts before revealing the rest of her body. As she stripped him, he could not wait for the bath and immediately penetrated her. This led to them soaking in the tub, washing each other thoroughly and enjoying each other again. It was approaching dawn when Jack said he had a plane to catch so she left with his promise that he would call. Shawna did not go to work and went home to sleep. To her delight, Jack did call when his plane landed telling her how he loved their evening together and hoped he could visit soon. As he shared the list of football games he would be attending, he mentioned that she could drive to the school where he would be in three weeks. As Shawna managed her daily workload and helped Maggie at the house, her heart and mind were focused on Jack's next visit. Jack also called her regularly to share where he had been, along with recounting their first night together and his anticipation of their second night, including a romantic dinner.

When the day of their second meeting arrived, Shawna drove to the school where Jack was scouting and they sat close together in the cool air with their usual banter and laughter. Jack showed Shawna how he was tracking the players and how his company would make offers to the best players to guide their football careers. The restaurant Jack chose was upscale with delicious food and when they reached the hotel room, Jack carried her across the threshold like a bride and wasted no time unwrapping her and himself. As before, they engaged each other the entire night and as dawn approached, Jack got ready to catch his plane. He walked her to her car, kissed her passionately while slipping his hand under her blouse and bra suggesting seriously he could penetrate her one last time in the back of her car. A call on his phone stopped him and, as he rushed away, he looked back several times and waved as he disappeared into the driver's seat. Shawna, so filled with satisfaction, did not want to leave the spot. This time, she had taken a vacation day so she felt no guilt as she slept and dreamed of her lover. Myrna by this time was expecting her second baby and Rachael was four years old. Shawna's parents, Katie and Randy, invited everyone to their house regularly. Shawna looked forward to the day when she could take Jack and announce their wedding plans.

For a year or so, Shawna and Jack had several rendezvous, all with the same banter, laughter and physical intensity. One afternoon at work, Shawna got a call from an unknown number and she let it go into voice mail. Her mind and body froze as she listened to the first four words of the message: "This is Jack's wife." Shawna called Jack and it went into voice mail. She asked him to call but he didn't. The next day, Jack's wife called again; Shawna blocked her. And that was the end of Jack. Shawna, somewhat shell-shocked, moved on like the year never happened, transferring all her focus and energy into her work with twelve-hour days, sometimes seven days per week. After a few years, this resulted in promotion to store manager and a salary that afforded her a condo of her own.

Being a manager brought Shawna invitations to conventions attended by other managers from every state in the country. In this world she found the elite class of men in tailored dark suits with current style shirts and ties, manicures and professional haircuts. At one of the sessions, she sat next to a lean, tall man with thinning hair and structured face. The intensity of his blue eyes was striking as he introduced himself, 'Glenn', with outstretched hand and a smile. At a break, he walked with her for a beverage saying what state he was from and he was married with two grown children. After a few more words, it was obvious he followed Jesus. When the session ended, he invited her to dine with him and they ate at the hotel restaurant.

"Why don't you believe in Jesus, Shawna?" Glenn finally asked, which was probably the reason for the dinner.

"I don't 'not' believe in him," Shawna explained. "I've never been interested in church and all their regulations."

"You know he's very interested in you, don't you?" Glenn responded. "He wants to spend his life with you now and for eternity."

"How can you know that?" Shawna asked with some irritation. "You can't see him or hear him."

"He wrote it in the Bible," Glenn answered. "He answers prayers."

Shawna said no more and they finished in silence, each going to their rooms. The next day, Glenn was in his seat and he again walked with her for a beverage at break and invited her to dinner, but she declined. She instead got takeout and watched a movie in her room, glad that she would be going home in the morning.

The next few years rolled by with Myrna's children now eight and four and Myrna expecting her third. She posted on social media the new house they were building. Myrna was a slim beauty who had just turned thirty and Keith was handsome and healthy; the picture-perfect family.

Shawna had gained fifty pounds, probably from her love, no, her need, of alcohol every night and her choice of easy fast food. Although she met all kinds of men through the days and weeks, none of the encounters resulted in a date much less a relationship.

In a mirror one day, Shawna became shockingly aware of the change age had made in her face and body. It was the first time she noticed a second, unattractive chin and this led her to admitting that she was overweight. Finding a fitness center that was open 24/7, she stopped every night to walk on the treadmill and lift some weights. She also found the resolve to avoid alcohol and keep healthy food in her fridge. After a year, she was happy with the size clothes she could wear and the lessening of the second chin.

The fitness center staff came and went throughout the year and most of the time they were cordial and helpful but not personal. This changed one night when a new guy, Jon, in mid twenties maybe, asked Shawna 'get-acquainted' questions. After talking several minutes, Shawna broke away to work out. Then, every night when Shawna arrived, Jon asked about her day and listened with interest and sometimes with sympathy anything Shawna shared. Naturally wondering if Jon was interested in her, she watched him as he interacted with other customers and decided he was not treating her special. One could imagine, though, that spending a shift in a fitness center from 10 PM to daybreak would be boring for a young man, and he passed the time chatting with everyone as they worked out. As he was standing by Shawna one night, he bent down and touched her leg showing her how it should be positioned. Evidently, when she expressed gratitude, he took it as permission to become her trainer which gave him permission to touch what he wanted to touch. Shawna, liking the attention, did not object, and the touches became obviously sexual. One night, as he pressed his groin on her buttocks to demonstrate how to bend properly, he told her he had a pamphlet in his office. She followed him there where he closed the door, dropped his pants and offered her a taste of his swollen bulge. She accepted and

Jon became her lover, teacher and coach, not only walking her through a routine but counseling her on her attitude toward herself and her lifestyle habits. He showed her workout clothes he liked and she wore them for him. She noticed everything that made him smile or not smile and changed accordingly. Several months passed when Shawna was then greeted by a new girl at the counter who said Jon had graduated from college and went home. And that was the end of Jon. Shawna, somewhat shell-shocked, moved on like the last few months hadn't happened, remembered Jon's lifestyle advice and forced herself to work out.

Chapter 3

Of all the heartaches Shawna had experienced, none hurt so much as the passing of her father, Randy. Though in his mid-sixties, he suffered a major heart attack and died instantly. As friends and family gathered at Katie's house, Shawna marveled at her growing nieces and nephew: Rachael now twelve, Ryan, eight, and Little Katie, almost four. Shawna also admired the glow of happiness that surrounded Myrna and Kevin; how they moved in unison; how they smiled at each other and he gently touched her arm, stroking it softly. When Myrna spoke, every word had Kevin's attention. Shawna knew she was observing the 'something more' that Myrna spoke of years ago.

When friends left the house, Katie, Shawna, Myrna and Kevin talked about where Katie should live. Katie didn't want to leave the house while Myrna expressed concern about Katie being alone. When Katie didn't disagree with Myrna, Shawna offered to move in, which everyone agreed with. So, selling her condo and investing the proceeds, Shawna settled in with her mother.

In addition, because the financial and customer satisfaction statistics of Shawna's store were excellent, she was made manager of a district of six stores with a staff of six. For the first few months, Shawna worked her usual long hours training her staff to achieve excellence in their stores. If she saw statistics improving in a store, she felt confident that the manager was effectively following her procedures so she did not have to spend much time with that manager, and chose to spend the extra hours in the evening with her mom. In time, only one of the stores had repeated problems so she was able to concentrate her day in that area and even got some weekends off. This was when Shawna realized that her mom was following Jesus earnestly, not only praying over food and attending church, but avoiding secular programs and reading the Bible or books about the Bible. When Shawna marveled that her mom was interested in 'that stuff', Katie responded that she had a 'born-again'[4] experience where God touched her spirit and filled her with a desire to please him[5]. Katie further explained that God was pleased when she prayed, read and followed the Bible and avoided the secular world.

The next morning, Shawna headed to her problematic store where she felt the root cause was lack of respect for rules and lack of respect for each other. The company's upper management frowned on firing employees, and asking for termination required egregious behavior or circumstances. Besides, firing an uncooperative employee didn't guarantee they would be replaced with a cooperative one. Upon arrival, Shawna met with the store manager and Shawna let her talk for quite a while. Then, if the manager's issues were structural or mechanical, they visited the site and decided on resolution. If the issue involved people, they had meetings. Of the three people they met with, one of them was extremely troubling to Shawna and she shared the situation with her mom, Katie. When Katie suggested prayer, Shawna ended the conversation, silently scoffing at her mother's beliefs.

At the store the next day, Shawna decided to work side-by-side with the uncooperative employee to show him what he needed to do. She found him to be rude, obnoxious, defiant and not productive in any degree. It didn't take long for him to object to her presence and her instructions. He flung a heavy box toward her which she dodged then he claimed it was an accident. She called for security and a couple of guys showed up. Shawna picked up the box, handed it to the employee and repeated her instruction. Then she realized that this had become a game of 'chicken', where he wasn't going to back down. So she backed down and left with the security officers following them to their office where she instructed them to tape the employee. The tape the next day showed him moving slowly, resting often, disappearing often, and ranting at associates. With a copy of the tape downloaded onto her computer tablet, she called for the employee, the store manager and a security officer.

"What are you doing here, Ross?" Shawna asked, pointing to her tablet where Ross was sitting on a pile of boxes.

"It's a break," Ross replied with a shrug. "Don't I get a break?"

"Where are you here then?" Shawna asked pointing to him being nowhere.

"I hadda pee," Ross snickered. "Don't I get a pee?"

"What are you doing here?" Shawna asked pointing to Ross ranting at a stunned associate.

"Oh man! That dumbass!" Ross cried. "He don't know nothin'. I told him a hundred times not to do that and he did it anyway!"

"Ross," Shawna began seriously, "this company doesn't want to fire people, but you have done enough in this tape that they would let me fire you."

"Hell, I been fired before," Ross scoffed. "I'll get me six weeks' unemployment and find another stinking' job."

"Listen to me," Shawna began as she clutched his shoulder. "I started out like you. I worked the floor for eight boring hours with dumb associates and dumb customers. But, you know what? Now I manage six stores and make a ton of money. I've got thousands of dollars in savings. I can go where I want and do what I want. But do you know what I want to do?"

"Uh-uh," Ross uttered shaking his head, mesmerized at Shawna's talk of money.

"I want to help you," Shawna answered, staring directly into Ross' face, eventually making him turn away. "Does any job in this store interest you?"

"Sports, I guess," Ross muttered with a sigh.

"Can you give me four weeks of good behavior?" Shawna asked with her hand still on his shoulder, looking into his eyes.

Ross shrugged his shoulders, looking down.

"Give me four weeks of not attacking associates; not sitting on the job; not disappearing and I'll move you to sports," Shawna offered.

"Sports and paint are covered together," the store manager added.

"OK, you have to take care of paint," Shawna agreed. "You can do both, right?"

Ross shrugged and Shawna rose to escort Ross out the door.

"You can do this, Ross," Shawna declared. "You don't have to settle for unemployment and another stinkin' job. I'll see you in four weeks."

On the way home, Shawna felt good about her conversation with Ross and confident it would have a good outcome. It was dark and a lightening bolt streaked across the sky with thunder close behind and torrents of rain. As she exited the freeway, her headlights revealed a car stretched across the road and the eyes of a horrified passenger knowing he was about to be hit. Shawna jerked the steering wheel to the left to avoid a head-on into the passenger but a car behind her plowed head-on into her.

The next day, Shawna woke up in a hospital bed, not able to move.

"Mom," Shawna said softly and Katie rushed to her bedside.

"Thank you, Lord!" Katie exclaimed with tears escaping then she touched Shawna's shoulder. "We almost lost you."

"I can't move," Shawna murmured.

"Not surprising," Katie responded with a sad smile. "I think every bone you have is broken."

"What about the others?" Shawna asked.

"Bumps and bruises, probably concussions, but all treated and released," Katie reported. "I need to tell Myrna that you're awake; she's been frantic."

Katie turned away and Shawna started wondering about the stores.

"Has the store called?" Shawna asked when Katie got off the phone.

"Yes, Mr. Donaldson?" Katie answered. "He said you were not to worry. He met with the six store managers and he was pleased with how they were handling their stores. They sent flowers and there are about a hundred cards."

Katie brought over a large basket of flowers, almost half as tall as Katie.

"What did the doctor say?" Shawna asked, unimpressed by the flowers.

"You will probably be here a week then you can go home," Katie began. "In two or three months, you will begin physical therapy."

Myrna, Kevin and the children came in and they spent the rest of the day planning Shawna's recovery. It did take all of three months for Shawna to start to lift weights with her arms and legs. She was complimented often that her body was in good shape and Shawna silently thanked Jon, her self-appointed trainer. In another month, she had good control of her upper body and could walk with assistance of a walker. She was experiencing pain in her back, though, that made her not want to walk. Doctors were not surprised at her complaint but they were unsure of the cause. Making the pain go away might be accomplished with surgery but there was no guarantee. Not wanting to risk surgery, Shawna came to the conclusion that she could no longer work at the discount store. The store agreed to pay her long term disability and she made a visit to each of her stores to say good-bye. Myrna drove her and walked around the stores with her.

"Ross," Shawna said as she and her walker hobbled up to him in the sports section.

"Miss Shawna!" Ross greeted with a smile and outstretched hands.

Shawna turned it into a gentle hug.

"Look at you!" Shawna beamed, "And look at this section. It looks fantastic!"

"I'm so glad to have the chance to thank you, Ma'am," Ross stated. "So glad! I was very sad to hear about the accident."

"Let's see the paint section," Shawna diverted and moved in that direction.

Ross walked proudly beside Shawna as she complimented his work. Shawna glanced at the store manager who also looked very pleased.

"What else interests you?" Shawna ventured, again looking at the store manager.

"Men's clothes?" Ross grinned with excitement.

Shawna turned to the store manager who nodded approval.

"Men's clothes it is, My Friend," Shawna announced and she reached out to hug him again.

"God be with you, Miss Shawna," Ross whispered.

Before Shawna left the store, she asked the store manager to try to steer Ross to the career improvement courses. When they got in the car, Myrna asked about Ross, and Shawna shared the backstory.

"That's impressive, Shawna," Myrna stated. "To influence people like that - it's a wonderful gift from God."

"What good does that do now?" Shawna retorted with anger as tears welled. "Why did God take this from me?"

"He has his reasons," Myrna answered softly. "It could be he wants you to use your talent for him and not for a secular store. You have to ask him."

When Shawna got home, she went to her room, which had to be moved to the first floor because climbing the stairs was too painful. Laying on the bed, she let her sadness break into deep sobs.

"Why did you take this from me?" Shawna asked God, as Myrna suggested, and she cried herself to sleep.

"The focus is Jesus," came the soft, audible answer a few hours later and Shawna could feel power in the words as they bombarded her black, cavernous spirit, exploding it into a wondrous, golden light.

"Yes," Shawna said as she rose up to a sitting position.

Opening the door into the living room, her mom was coming out of the kitchen.

"I'm born-again, Mom," Shawna announced with a smile.

With a squeal of delight, Katie bounded to her daughter embracing her warmly and Shawna described what happened.

Chapter 4

As Shawna got familiar with the Bible and avoided the secular world, God became more and more real to her and she thanked him often throughout the day for Jesus, for his sacrifice that absolved her of her sin nature[6], and for the Holy Spirit who leads and guides her[7]. As she was looking at Myrna's old social media posts: her wedding, her first house, first child and her current family pictures, Shawna realized how sin had robbed Shawna of years of happiness. Perhaps, if her parents had fought harder to protect her, she would have chosen a man like Keith or maybe remained a virgin. But, by following sin instead of Jesus, Shawna slept with the first man who approached her rather than waiting for a Godly man who would have partnered with her and who would be a conduit for God's love. By following sin instead of Jesus, Shawna left Rick, who loved her in his weird way. If she had been following Jesus, she would have stayed with Rick, and she could be enjoying Rick's attentions today, as shallow as they were. She might have eventually led Rick to Jesus which would have changed their relationship and lifestyle. While Shawna realized that God had given her more than enough, she was honest with God about wanting the true love that had been stolen from her. She prayed for God's will to be done, though, no matter what her feelings were.

One afternoon, God gave Shawna a romantic story to write, which she published, although it didn't get many sales. This story was about a single Christian man who was attracted to an unbeliever[8] at his job and, no matter how much he prayed, he could not erase his interest. He was determined to not become romantically involved with the unbeliever and avoided all contact with her. He even got himself transferred to another department to avoid her. Many times, as he prayed for his deliverance, he wept for her salvation. This went on for many months until, one Sunday, she walked down the aisle of his church to answer an altar call. With wonder and amazement, he walked behind her to hear her prayer of repentance and he knelt with thanksgiving at this gift God had given him. He marveled the rest of his life how the love of God poured through him to this woman, his wife.

Like the man, Shawna could not erase a desire for love in her life but, looking at herself in the mirror: looking older than her fifty years, a little chubby with that disgusting second chin, she could not see how any man could be interested in her. Like the Christian man in her story, though, she could not erase the idea that, if God gave her to a man as a wife, the love of God would flow through him to her.

God then blessed Shawna with ideas for a book about store and people management, which was published, and the discount store carried it. The company's upper management, impressed with the fresh content and wisdom, not to mention Shawna's real track record, hired her to train via webinars and invited her to speak at their country-wide conventions. To her surprise, Glenn, from that convention long ago, was waiting for her as she exited the stage after a talk. She accepted his invitation to dinner. He was widowed now, grandfather of four and was overjoyed to hear that Shawna was following Jesus. They spent the rest of the evening talking about her accident and her conversion. When they said 'good-night', Shawna smiled at their time together and wondered if they would meet again. The next Sunday at her church, as Shawna waited in the church pew for the service to begin, she stared with wonder and amazement as Glenn stood at the end of the pew and asked, 'Is this seat taken?'. She reached her hand to him which he took and held the entire service. During the message, as they glanced at each other, their heads automatically came together for a soft kiss.

After the service, Shawna introduced Glenn to her mom, Myrna and her family. Rather than having Sunday dinner with them, Shawna and Glenn ate together. Glenn explained that his wife had died a few years after he met Shawna, and his grief for his wife's passing kept him from seeking a new relationship. Thankfully, his life was filled with escorting his two children through their college years, their marriages and the birth of his grandchildren. Then, even though they involved him in their lives, he wanted to again experience loving a wife.

"When you were on the stage at the convention, something like a warm breeze started flowing through me," Glenn explained. "I felt like, if I connected with you, it would flow through me to you."

Shawna then shared the romantic story she had written and her prayer for love in her life.

"For you to show up at my church like you did," Shawna marveled, looking to Heaven with thanksgiving, "you had to be a gift from God. There could be no other explanation."

At that moment, Shawna could feel herself becoming one with Glenn in spirit and she had no misgivings about her age, her past or her double chin. Their conversation turned to planning a small wedding ceremony with family only and where they would live. They decided to keep both houses for now because of Katie, Shawna's mom, in her eighties, and because Glenn's home was in a warm climate. After their wedding, they flew to Glenn's home and arrived late, on purpose, so they could have the night to themselves. Glenn parked the bags in the bedroom and led Shawna to a couch in a cozy family room. Putting his arm on her shoulder behind her head, he asked God to bless their union and to lead and guide them in their marriage. He then caressed her waiting lips. Before going further, he expressed embarrassment that he was not a strapping young stud anymore and she laughed, saying she had the same concern. Slipping her hand under his belt and into his briefs, she announced that God's plumbing seemed to be working fine. From there, passion took over. Though their passion did not have the energy of their youth, the love of God flowing through them intensified their physical reactions. As Shawna lay beside Glenn, studying him, she felt complete and secure. She felt loved.

In the next year, Shawna and Glenn formed a Christian group for discount store employees, meeting over the internet to pray, study the

Bible and help however they could. Shawna's gift of influence led many to follow Jesus earnestly. At the discount store conventions, members of the Christian group met for dinner, and seeing Ross at a convention his first year as store manager was a joy that Shawna could not adequately express.

Though Glenn and Shawna enjoyed each other physically for many years, they realized that the love of God flowing through them was just as intense without physical actions. It warmed Shawna's heart that pictures of herself, Glenn and his family were now added to Myrna's social media account. As Jesus said, "The thief cometh not, but for to steal, and to kill, and to destroy: I am come that they might have life, and that they might have it more abundantly.[9]"

Her Kind of Fun
Chapter 1

When your spirit is dead, you will do what you can to feel alive. Lucky people feel alive loving their family be it their parents, siblings, spouse or children, or they may devote their lives to their career, their hobbies, their beliefs, etc. Unlucky ones feel alive hurting themselves or others as in stealing, killing, addiction or abuse, to name only a few options. Catherine was abusive.

Catherine's power to abuse was derived from how her body formed in the womb. The pieces and parts came together in a combination that the world called 'beautiful', 'stunning', or 'gorgeous'. Along with the physical came the talent and desire to enhance and heighten the beauty. In other words, Catherine chose tasteful, complimentary outfits plus she liked foods that maintained the correct body weight and nourished her hair and skin. In addition, though she wasn't an athlete, she liked moving her body, preferably by social dancing, but also by physical activities like tennis or swimming.

Catherine's affluent parents basked with pride in how she looked, showing her off in as many beauty pageants and parades as possible. They learned early to anticipate what she wanted or to give in to her demands. Eventually their family activities and vacations were based on what Catherine wanted to do, and Catherine's response to their generosity and acquiescence was to hate them: to ignore school requirements, to party all night, sometimes not coming home, and to begin sexual relations in her early teens. Men became Catherine's drug of choice and not only because of the physical sexual act, but the entire process of dressing to attract a man, flirting with him, arousing him and then experiencing the strength of his body. In addition to the physical ecstasy, the man's intense focus temporarily revived her dead spirit.

In spite of Catherine's behavior and very poor grade average, her parents got her into a college that put them deep in debt, and they let her choose where she wanted to live. After they helped her furnish a house on campus, Catherine expressed relief that she would finally be rid of them, even though, with her constant requests for money, they did not get rid of her. Howard, who eventually became Catherine's husband, was an incoming freshman like Catherine and lived in the house next door, though he had several roommates, mostly football players. Catherine's beauty caught their attention of course and most of them fell all over themselves to become acquainted. Naturally, she took advantage, using them for routine maintenance like mowing the lawn or fixing a leaky faucet, and, in exchange, she let them have parties at her place. Howard, however, kept his distance and didn't attend the parties which made him a challenge Catherine intended to overcome. Though Catherine was sexually active, she was able to present herself to Howard, not as a virgin, but as someone with morals. He never knew otherwise because she chose sex partners who were not associated with the school and who were not going to pursue a relationship.

In her sophomore year, Catherine's dad, who followed the college football games, predicted that Howard would be picked up by one of the national football organizations and be worth millions of dollars. Seeing Howard as a gold mine, Catherine managed to lure him into her house to help with studies or something, offering to cook dinner sometime. Eventually he accepted her invitation where she lavished him with attention and demurely asked questions about anything that interested him. When he informed her that he followed Jesus and he was deeply interested in God and the Bible, Catherine should have walked away; but the lure of his looming wealth was too powerful.

Eventually, Howard and Catherine were seen as a couple on campus and in the community, and his buddies adopted her as their team mascot, welcoming her as 'good luck' on the sidelines and in the locker room. Though coaches didn't like it, the team was winning so they let it go.

Catherine's parents burst with pride as she was pictured with Howard on national TV shows and sometimes asked questions; Catherine's social media account had thousands of followers. With all of this attention, you would think Catherine's dead spirit would feel alive but she found a way to be unhappy: Howard would not take her to bed, and she was not able to connect to a lover because it was highly probable that Media would discover and report any infidelity. The situation was forcing Catherine to give up something she wanted: either she abstain from sex or give up the gold mine, Howard. Fortunately for Catherine, Howard started talking about marriage, and when Howard proposed, Catherine took his gorgeous ring, comforting herself that, as his wife, she could have both sex and money. After that, with her dad's credit card, she was able to shop for the wedding which kept her dead spirit occupied and fulfilled.

Catherine invited her cousin Nora to be maid-of-honor, and Nora was excited to accept. As cousins the same age, Catherine and Nora were drawn to each other at the many family functions, growing closer as they got older. When they were given access to text and social media, they stayed in constant contact on an intimate level. Catherine disclosed when she gave away her virginity; Nora disclosed when she answered an altar call at church and said the 'sinner's prayer'. After Catherine met Howard, she took him to one of the family functions. As the star quarterback on his college team, he was greeted enthusiastically which he graciously received. As he answered questions and diverted praise to his coaches and teammates, Catherine observed that Nora was interested in Howard and envious. Seeing the opportunity to torture Nora, Catherine invited Nora to shopping sprees on her dad's credit card and lunches with a few of her old friends and some of her new. Though Catherine's new friends acted graciously, their professionally styled hair, makeup, jewelry and clothing were intimidating to Nora, because the difference in the cousins' appearance was striking. Everything about Catherine's face was perfect: the size of her dark brown eyes and the straight bridge of her nose leading to lips of medium thickness that did not need artificial color; all surrounded by smooth, creamy skin and dark hair with soft highlights. Her top revealed the fullness of her breasts that made you imagine a man's desire to touch them. In contrast, Nora's breasts were as full but the same size as her waist, and she was a head shorter with mousy brown, naturally frizzy hair. In addition, it was noticeable that Nora's nose dipped down somewhat like a witch's.

At Catherine's bachelor party where champaign flowed freely and catered hors d'oeuvres abounded, Catherine revealed with giggles that Howard would not take her to bed until their wedding night. When the girls insisted on intimate details, Catherine said she didn't know if he was a virgin, and she had never seen him naked so she could only guess from the bulge in his swim trunks what she might expect. This of course led to not only wedding night tales but 'first time' tales, both romantic and disastrous. For Nora, who listened quietly, it was a lesson in an activity she had yet experienced. She wondered, if Howard was a virgin, was he also a Christian, and, if he was a Christian, why did he choose Catherine, an unbeliever[10]?

When Howard graduated from college, he was chosen by a professional football team, eventually landing a multi-million dollar contract, as Catherine's dad had predicted. Catherine's posts now included behind the scene shots of media personalities and functions. Her selfies included Howard in tuxedos and herself in luxurious evening gowns. Their wedding pictures were blasted all over national media.

Chapter 2

The first morning as Howard's wife, reality fell on Catherine like she was a building that had been bombed. As she sat across from Howard sipping coffee, nothing she saw interested her. Though Catherine wasn't aware of it, with Howard's body at her beck and call, the extended thrill of dressing, attracting, arousing and experiencing a man was gone. When Howard tried to make conversation, he withdrew at Catherine's sullen, one-word responses, and became quiet. This is when she discovered a new pastime to revive her dead spirit - hurting Howard. Deciding that she wanted sexual attention, she put on her bikini and dove into the pool to swim laps. Predictably, Howard came out to watch her and, when she got out of the pool, she walked close enough for him to touch her, which he did. He gently took her hand to guide her onto his lap followed by giggles, kisses and caresses. Though this attention was what she wanted, it was over too soon, and he left for a team meeting. With no intention of spending the afternoon alone, she showered and dressed deciding to have lunch at a private club; finding herself a lover, she texted Howard that she was spending the night with a friend.

At the team meeting, Howard's distress at the text was noticeable, and Rodney, Howard's friend and the team's unofficial chaplain, asked Howard if he was alright.

"It's Catherine," Howard began. "She's staying with a friend tonight."

"A friend?" Rodney questioned, knowing there were rumors of Catherine's infidelity.

"Yeah," Howard chuckled sadly, then he sighed deeply, putting his head in his hands. "If she's bored with me after one night, will the marriage be over in a week?"

"That's up to you, isn't it?" Rodney counseled. "You said you were asking God to change her, right? Are you giving up on him after one night?"

"I've been praying for four years," Howard whined.

"And in those four years, you could have walked away!" Rodney exclaimed. "No-one held a gun to your head! Her beauty captured you and, apparently, she put on an act that you believed. Don't tell me the Holy Spirit didn't warn you.[11]"

Howard's body shot back, slamming against the back of the chair, looking to Heaven, as though Rodney had struck him.

"You're right," Howard murmured. "I should have walked away; I should have run away; I should have moved far, far away."

"She's your wife now and you're commanded to love her,[12]" Rodney continued. "You vowed, before God, to stay with her until death parts you, for better or worse. Every day will be torture for you, I'm sure; and, at the same time, you can't let down the team. Only God can help you, My Friend. It would not surprise me at all that God allowed you to marry Catherine just so you would be completely dependent on him."

Howard nodded in agreement, and they knelt to ask God for his help, his strength and his wisdom.

The next week, Nora, responding to a text from Catherine, was sitting in the luxurious living room with a floor to ceiling window overlooking a massive manicured landscape, and could barely withhold her distain as Catherine whined about her life. Catherine said her life was dull because, when Howard was not with the football team, he was happy cooking, reading and watching sports. She added that, because he did not accept any of the invitations they received for parties and other events, she had no social life, unless it was to visit the sick in hospitals or attend charity fundraisers occasionally.

At this point, Howard entered the room having returned from a team practice; he walked directly to Catherine, bent down and gently kissed her lips when she looked up at him. She immediately turned her head away from him and looked down with a grimace.

"Nora, isn't it?" he said to Nora, seemingly ignoring Catherine's reaction and offering his hand.

"Right," Nora smiled, taking his hand and added. "Howard, isn't it?"

"Right," he laughed. "I'm surprised you remembered."

"Oh, not that hard when your father never misses a game or an interview or a documentary or..." Nora taunted.

"Ok, that's enough," Howard demanded with a smile then turned back to Catherine. "Hungry for anything special?"

"Uh-uh," she murmured shaking her head, still frowning.

"I'll see what I can find," he replied, gently rubbing her shoulder.

Watching him walk toward the kitchen, Nora pictured herself walking beside or behind him, wanting to be next to him whatever he did. Her mind wandered toward what he might look like in the shower, then she rose immediately to tell Catherine she had to leave.

"Can't we go out?" Catherine asked with pleading in her eyes.

"Do you need me to go out with you?" Nora questioned.

"I don't have a car but it will be fun," Catherine insisted. "You deserve a little fun, don't you?"

"Going out" to Catherine meant going to a club and drinking which Christians weren't supposed to do, but Nora accepted the invitation thinking this would cheer up Catherine. Catherine bounded off the couch and led Nora into her room. Like a couple of teenagers, they spent the next two hours choosing outfits from Catherine's massive walk-in closet and fixing their hair and makeup. Catherine's demeanor now was the complete opposite of the sullen, whiney woman on the couch. Then, without saying 'good-bye' to Howard, they piled into Nora's car and Catherine directed Nora to the club. Immediately hitting the dance floor, Catherine paired up with anyone who came close to her. Finding a table close by, Nora ordered a soft drink and a slice of pizza, then watched the mass of people move their bodies to the music or respond to the DJ's demands to lift their hands up or shake their booties. It was a while before Catherine found Nora and she brought a young man, Freddie, to join them. Freddie's brown hair, topped with a fedora, touched his shoulders which were covered with a silver scarf, setting off his dark blue polyester suit with a shirt underneath that allowed a glimpse of his tattooed chest. Black rimmed glasses with tinted lenses covered his eyes. Catherine's attraction to him as a rebellion against normal, boring Howard made perfect sense to Nora. Watching Catherine flirt with Freddie saddened Nora knowing Catherine should now be flirting with her husband. Flirting with Howard would definitely be Nora's choice based on the information she had. Nora guessed it would be possible that other things were happening behind closed doors that Catherine wasn't sharing.

In the months to come, Catherine texted about Freddie and the parties she managed to sneak to, but, about four months after Catherine met Freddie, her texts stopped; Nora got worried and stopped to see her.

"Nora," Howard greeted with a frown as he answered the door.

"I was worried about Catherine," Nora explained immediately, seeing his displeasure.

"I...I don't want you to see her," Howard stated honestly. "I think you are a bad influence."

"What's wrong?" Nora asked with worry about Catherine, ignoring Howard's accusation.

"Nora?" Catherine cried from a distance.

"I don't want you to see her," Howard repeated urgently as Nora walked passed him; he followed saying, "I'm not leaving you alone with her."

Walking into the luxurious living room where Catherine and Nora had met before, Nora saw the back of Catherine's head as she faced the floor-to-ceiling window. As Nora approached Catherine's dark hair, her lovely face came into view then her swollen abdomen.

"You're pregnant?" Nora blurted as she knelt beside Catherine.

"Obviously," Catherine fumed, jerking her head toward Howard. "And Knucklehead won't pay for an abortion."

"It's a gift from God!," Howard blurted. "Abortion is murder."

"Being pregnant is murder!" Catherine exclaimed and she again jerked her head toward Howard. "Being his wife is murder!"

Howard was facing the window with his hands in his pockets.

"Let's go to my room," Catherine suggested.

"No," Howard stated firmly. "No more secrets, Catherine."

"What secrets?" Nora found herself saying, though she usually minded her own business.

"Tell her, Catherine," Howard demanded firmly.

"It's not his baby," Catherine announced, glaring at him with an air of victory, happy to be hurting him.

Nora looked at Howard with wonder, who was still looking out the window, because he was not aborting the baby and he was not divorcing Catherine.

"What else?" Howard continued.

"I was paying Freddie's rent, car payment and utilities on Howard's credit card," Catherine added with a giggle. "Thousands of dollars before Knucklehead found it. Oh, we had some good times!"

A deep sigh escaped from Howard and he turned to Nora.

"She met Freddie the night she went out with you," Howard stated factually. "I don't want you around her."

"He's saying that to all my friends!" Catherine wailed.

"You have to let me see her," Nora insisted. "I understand that you don't trust me but I don't trust you, and I want to know that she's alright."

"I'll keep in touch," Howard offered.

"No!" Nora bellowed. "You let me see her or I'll contact social services! I'll stop by every day after work."

"Every day?" Howard bellowed back.

"It's me or them!" Nora roared then stomped toward the door to leave.

The first night Nora stopped by, Howard led her to Catherine who was sitting on that same couch. The house was filled with a pleasant aroma of something cooking and some kind of horror movie was playing on the wall-mounted big screen.

"You need to get me out of here," Catherine begged.

"Why?" Nora asked, truly wanting to know Catherine's reasons. "You seem to be safe here. You seem to be eating and wanting for nothing. Who is cleaning and washing your clothes?"

"Knucklehead hired someone," Catherine muttered.

"Stop calling him that!" Nora blurted, wanting to protect Howard. "Don't call him names! Even if he is abusing you, it's wrong to call him names. Is he abusing you?"

"Making me have this baby is abuse!" Catherine exclaimed. "Making me be his wife is abuse!"

"Making you have the baby is the right thing to do," Nora retorted. "How is being his wife abusive?"

"I hate him!" Catherine raged.

"Why?" Nora challenged. "There has to be a reason for this hatred."

Howard appeared saying that supper was ready and Nora rose to leave.

"You can't leave!" Catherine wailed, taking hold of Nora's arm.

"I'll be back tomorrow after work," Nora assured her. "You'll be alright. Nothing here is hurting you."

"You're welcome to stay," Howard offered with tenderness so different from yesterday.

It took all of Nora's strength not to embrace him; she was longing for him to hold her and love her instead of Catherine. Nora's disdain for Catherine's self-centered, selfish attitude had increased a hundred-fold as well as her admiration and sympathy for Howard. Because of a fortuitous text from her mom, Nora broke out of her trance and declined the invitation, moving quickly toward the door.

The next night, Nora arrived and Howard introduced her to Rodney, a Christian friend. Howard led Nora to Catherine in her room and left. Catherine was in bed, not dressed, with matted, uncombed hair.

"What's going on?" Nora asked, kneeling beside Catherine.

"I want to die," Catherine murmured. "I can't live like this."

"Like what?" Nora challenged.

"Like a prisoner," Catherine muttered.

"Listen to me," Nora begged. "You are not a prisoner but walking out of here is the dumbest thing I ever heard. You have everything anyone could possibly want, including a hunk of a husband who is devoted to you in spite of your cheating. I see no evidence that he is hurting you. What I do see is a very confused person."

Catherine turned away from Nora.

"Have you talked to your parents?" Nora asked.

"They are in Europe," Catherine murmured. "They aren't answering me."

"Where do you think you can go then?" Nora continued. "If you go to my parent's house, they will help you until the baby is born but then they will expect you to get a job and take care of yourself. Is that what you want?"

"I don't want the baby," Catherine blubbered.

"Look, here's the problem," Nora concluded, getting irritated. "You are a spoiled, self-centered child. If I were you, I would ask God for help and pray that Howard continue to put up with you. If I were you, I would pray the sinner's prayer."

This ended the conversation with Catherine pulling covers over her head. As Nora walked down the stairs, Howard stopped her; Rodney was waiting by the door.

"Thank you," Howard murmured.

"You need to pray for her," Nora suggested, still irritated.

"Yes, I pray for her," Howard responded with a sigh.

"Since the bachelor party, I wondered if you were a Christian," Nora stated mindlessly, moving toward the door.

"Why the bachelor party?" Howard questioned.

"Well, aaahhh, Catherine said you wouldn't take her to bed," Nora muttered, looking down, embarrassed. "I wondered if you were a Christian."

"Right," Howard affirmed. "That's how I was brought up and I came to understand why in my teens. That's when I confessed to my family and my church that I was following Jesus."

"So, you yoked yourself to an unbeliever[13]," Nora declared, "and reaped the consequences."

"Indeed I have," Howard agreed nodding, looking at Rodney, "but I vowed to love[14] her until death parts us."

"I think you should take Catherine out often so she can socialize," Nora suggested. "You may have to endure her drinking and flirting but you can at least keep her out of trouble and get her home safe."

"You don't know what you're asking," Howard whined looking to Heaven. "The press…"

"They aren't allowed everywhere," Nora interrupted. "There are private clubs."

"Expensive private clubs," Howard wailed.

"You made the choice; you pay the price," Nora reminded him and she left; Rodney followed her to her car.

"I know you're trying to help," Rodney began, "but you are promoting sin."

"I *am* trying to help," Nora agreed, "and you have to understand that Catherine has been spoiled her entire life. You can't expect her to suddenly be sinless."

"You have to be careful," Rodney continued with sincere concern. "She's a liar and a deceiver. I don't think she knows how to love anyone, not even herself."

The next time Nora visited, Rodney was there again and Catherine was in her room; a maid was helping her get dressed. The low cut, sparkling gown was designed to lessen the bump in her stomach. With styled hair and a touch of makeup, Catherine's beauty filled the room. Howard appeared in the door in black tailored jacket and pants with starched white shirt and black bow tie. His eyes sparkled as he studied Catherine.

"We're going to the Casbah!" Catherine exclaimed looking with pride at her gown in the mirror.

"You can thank..." Howard began.

"How wonderful!" Nora quickly interrupted, shaking her head at Howard.

"The car is here," Howard stammered.

Hugging Catherine, Nora wished her a wonderful evening then pushed Howard toward the front door.

"Don't tell her it was my idea!" Nora whispered to Howard.

"Really?" Howard answered innocently.

"She can do no wrong tonight, do you understand?" Nora lectured.

"Now, wait a minute," Howard objected, looking helplessly at Rodney.

"Let her have her kind of fun," Nora insisted. "You just keep her safe and out of trouble. Pray for her. Try to limit the alcohol for the baby's sake. Maybe pay the waitress to water down her drinks."

"What a waste of money," Howard complained.

"Your choice..." Nora repeated.

"I pay the price," Howard muttered, nodding. "I know."

Nora left and Rodney followed, again expressing his disagreement with Nora's suggestions.

"Have you talked to him?" Nora asked.

"A little," Rodney answered.

"Why did he marry her?" Nora pressed.

"She's beautiful, of course," Rodney chuckled, looking away from Nora. "He should have exercised self-control and stayed away from her, and he knows it now. He's paying the price for not following Jesus earnestly."

"What do you mean by 'earnestly'?" Nora questioned.

"If he had followed Jesus earnestly, he would have never gone to her house in the first place," Rodney answered, looking at Nora. "He would have never given her the chance to seduce him."

The next day, Catherine's happy texts and posts returned with pictures of the beautiful, wealthy Rich, male and female, she had met and danced with, and, when Nora visited, Catherine was doing fine. Then, in the kitchen, Howard didn't have much to say.

"You have to take her out again soon and you should start talking about it now," Nora demanded. "She'll need time to find a gown."

"How long will this go on?" Howard whined.

"Until God answers your prayers," Nora replied. "Where will you take her?"

"Pedros?" Howard suggested.

"Yes, good," Nora agreed. "Ask her when she wants to go then make the reservations."

Howard sighed and looked to Heaven.

"You can do this," Nora encouraged. "Remember, it's your idea. Are you slow dancing with her?"

Howard was silent.

"You aren't slow dancing with her?" Nora marveled.

"Al-Right!" Howard cried in surrender. "Slow dance it is."

Chapter 3

After a few months, the baby, Madeline, was born and a tiny, precious bundle she was. Wanting so badly to spend time with her, Nora invited her mom to visit, and they were delighted that Howard had found a Christian nurse and nanny, Anna. Feeling comfortable that the baby was in good hands, Nora checked on Catherine, sad to find her depressed again. This time it was the condition of her body causing the stress which was silly because she had the financial means to seek professional beauty experts and hire a physical trainer, in her home if she wished; Howard had his own training room. Once again, being the negotiator, Nora mentioned to Howard what Catherine needed. To her delight, he immediately called some team members to find out what salons and trainers their wives used. A few days later, Catherine invited Nora to her first salon visit and not only was the facility amazing but the staff was courteous, professional and knowledgable. Then, the next time Nora visited at Catherine's house, Catherine was in the training room following a fitness routine customized for her. Howard was working out also with a look of satisfaction; it was obvious he loved watching Catherine. As Nora started to fantasize about being watched by Howard, she left immediately to spend time with Madeline and Anna, the nanny.

For a year or so, Howard continued to take Catherine out regularly, and she continued her physical routines and salon visits. Nora and her mom stopped often to see Madeline and, many times, Rodney was there. Though Catherine never spent time with Madeline, Howard did, which warmed Nora's heart. Sadly, this peace was disrupted by another pregnancy and an ensuing argument over abortion. The father was a young salon employee and his parents wanted the child so Catherine had to fight three people instead of one. Beside herself with anger, Catherine threatened repeatedly to end her life. With Howard's permission, Nora spoke to her pastor and he asked for volunteers to form a 24/7 suicide and prayer watch over Catherine. Nora, with her mom or Rodney, watched from 6 PM to midnight, and it wasn't unusual at all to hear Howard weeping in his room. Rodney imagined he was praying for Catherine.

"I pray for you, Nora," Rodney confessed one evening, sitting across from her at the kitchen table.

"Thank you," Nora responded sincerely. "I appreciate that; I pray for you as well."

"What do you pray?" Rodney asked softly, looking down, obviously nervous.

"I pray for God's best for you; for his will to be done in you," Nora answered stiffly.

"You don't want to know what I pray for?" Rodney pressed gently but he didn't give Nora time to answer. "I pray for you to find your own husband. You are living your life through Catherine. Loving another woman's husband is wrong[15]."

"Yes, it is," Nora agreed, looking down, "and it's torture."

After a few days, Howard told Catherine he had arranged a night in Beverly Hills and, immediately snapping out of her depression, she asked if they could stay a couple of days, and she invited Nora to go. In spite of a warning from Rodney, Nora accepted the invitation. The private jet seated nine and during the few hours in the air, conversation flowed easily with a lot of 'get-acquainted' questions. Everyone either recognized Howard or knew of him as soon as he introduced himself. As the flight ended, Howard offered to buy dinner for everyone, and one of the passengers, Quentin, a film producer, accepted. The next day, Catherine, Quentin and Nora shopped the expensive stores on Rodeo Drive; Quentin became the guide and consultant. It was quite an experience with price tags Nora could barely fathom. Though Catherine tried to buy gifts for Nora, she declined furiously insisting she would return anything Catherine purchased. The gown Catherine chose was beyond gorgeous and would have fit in easily on any red carpet. Nora made Catherine buy Nora's gown at a second hand shop which was still outrageously expensive. That night, Catherine and Nora dressed in Nora's hotel room and, when they emerged, Howard was in the hall in his black evening suit; Quentin was with him. Catherine immediately struck a glamorous pose as the two men stared. Even though Catherine was pregnant, Quentin gasped and mouthed 'oh my god'.

At the club, after a five-star meal, Quentin and Catherine danced with anyone who got close to them. Howard was recognized and got into a lively sports conversation with a few guys. This was all fine until Quentin took Catherine in his arms for a slow dance. When Nora looked toward Howard, he was gone. Staying in the club with Catherine until the music stopped, Nora walked to her room along with everyone else, unaware that Quentin and Catherine were not following. Sleep came easily for Nora but after a few hours, there was a knock on the door, and Howard stood there, drunk.

"Catherine?" Howard asked in a low, begging tone.

Nora led him to a bed to lay down and he immediately started snoring. It broke Nora's heart that Catherine was, this very moment, choosing to caress someone else who didn't love her. Allowing herself to stroke Howard's thick black hair for a few seconds, Nora's heart ached for him; not only because of how Catherine treated him but also because Nora knew she could treat him better. Nora then laid down on a separate bed.

"What are you doing here?" Howard asked as he laid down next to Nora. "A wife should lay with her husband."

Nora started to rise and Howard clutched her then reached under Nora's top to caress her breasts.

"You're staying here with me." Howard blurted. "It's my turn."

"Howard!" Nora exclaimed. "This is Nora; not Catherine."

"That's a new one," Howard chuckled as he turned Nora toward him, imprisoning her with his strength, and pushed down her panties. "This belongs to me."

Howard touched the sensitive skin between her buttocks, and Nora gasped, losing her breath, as her groin caught fire and she shook with several spasms.

"Oh, my god," Nora whispered.

"Mmmmm," Howard crooned, touching her lips with his; mouthing her gently.

Though Nora was breathless and felt weak, she put her hands on his chest and pushed; trying to break his grasp. He took one of her hands and pushed it into his pants, under his briefs, to stroke his swollen bulge.

"For you, Wife," Howard whispered. "Only for you."

"Howard!" Nora cried. "I'm Nora! This is Nora!"

With one massive arm engulfing her, he got his pants pulled down then straddled her. As he continued to mouth her lips, he guided his bulge toward her groin. She pushed her hands against his chest and kicked as tears flowed freely.

"Howard! Howard!" she cried loudly, then she gasped again followed by a long, loud guttural groan as he inserted his bulge.

Once inserted, Howard began to thrust himself inside her, which was not like passion but like an attack; with every movement, groans from deep within Nora escaped. Though her body welcomed the electrifying sensation, tears flowed freely as she surrendered to the situation and waited for a chance to leave.

It came in a few minutes as the thrusts slowed to a stop and Howard withdrew himself; turning to lay on his back. Nora immediately rolled off the bed and, grabbing her suitcase, she rushed into the bathroom then locked the door. Though she wanted desperately to shower, she got dressed. When she emerged, Howard was snoring. Nora found her purse and left; not caring if anything was forgotten. Asking the concierge to get her a cab, she exchanged her ticket at the airport and flew home. At this point, she never wanted to see Howard or Catherine again.

The weeks following were torture as Nora could not erase the incident from her memory nor could she control the gamut of emotions ranging from the ecstasy of the physical act to the rage that it was done without her permission. All of this was heightened when she missed her period, and morphed into panic when she missed her next one. After consulting a doctor, Nora made an appointment for an abortion at a clinic many miles from her home, hoping no-one would ever find out. Every minute of every day, the Holy Spirit reminded her that Christians didn't get abortions; that abortion was murder; that she would regret the abortion the rest of her life. Nora knew that God wanted her to trust him and let him take care of her; but her faith in him was weak. All Nora could see was the chaotic effect this baby would have on Howard, Catherine and herself; all she could imagine was the baby being raised in an atmosphere of pain, confusion and anger.

On the day of the appointment, Nora parked and walked toward the clinic entrance.

"Nora," said a voice to Nora's right.

"What are you doing here?" Nora blurted to Rodney.

"I have the same question for you," Rodney replied with wonder.

"How did you know I would be here?" Nora exclaimed. "No-one knows."

"God knows," Rodney answered glibly. "The Holy Spirit knows and he led me here."

"He led you here?" Nora repeated incredulously.

"Yeah," Rodney responded, "but I didn't know why and I certainly didn't expect you to be here. Are you meeting someone?"

Nora shifted nervously and looked toward the clinic. She certainly didn't want to go in there but she believed she had no choice.

"I'm pregnant," Nora announced uncomfortably, wanting to end this conversation and get the abortion over with.

"With who?" Rodney demanded in disbelief.

"It's a long story," Nora stated as she turned toward the clinic. "I'm going to be late."

"Marry me!" Rodney demanded, and repeated in response to Nora's dumfounded look. "*Marry me.*"

Nora froze and stared at Rodney. On the surface, this was a perfect solution, then a thousand questions came to her mind; but, with a huge burden pulled off her soul, she texted the clinic to cancel the appointment.

"They will charge a cancellation fee," Nora murmured to herself.

"I'll pay it!" Rodney declared as he slowly walked toward her and gently took her arm. "Walk with me."

The clinic, in a park-like setting, was surrounded by a white, concrete walkway. A few people were walking or running.

"Who is the father?" Rodney began, looking ahead.

"It's hard to explain," Nora answered.

"A name is not hard to explain," Rodney insisted with irritation, then he sighed. "What happened?"

"It was in Beverly Hills..." Nora started.

"Of course," Rodney responded, looking toward Heaven. "Howard."

"Howard came to my room and he was drunk because Catherine was with another man," Nora continued firmly. "I felt sorry for him and let him in, and, as soon as he laid down, he started snoring."

"He..." Howard began then paused, sighing deeply, "raped you?"

"He didn't know it was rape!" Nora blurted. "He thought I was Catherine. If you ask him, he won't remember."

Rodney stopped walking, turned to Nora and put his hands on her shoulders.

"We'll have the baby together, alright?" Rodney continued. "It's God's baby and we'll raise it for him."

Nora nodded and, to her surprise, a warm feeling started flowing through Nora from Rodney. He pulled her into an embrace.

"With God's help, I'm going to love you, Nora," Rodney promised. "And I'm going to love God's baby, ok?"

Tears flowed as Nora nodded. Rodney held her for a long time.

Chapter 4

While nursing her newborn boy, Eddie, short for Edward, a name not associated with anyone's family, Nora should not have been shocked when she saw Catherine's post announcing a contract to publish a spread of nude photos in a men's magazine. After the birth of her second baby, Catherine had posted pictures in bikinis that left nothing to the imagination, along with her diet, exercise and beauty routines.

As Nora waited for Eddie to finish sucking, Rodney walked into the room, home from work, and sat on the couch next to her, cuddling close and resting his arm behind her head.

"I want it to be my turn," Rodney whispered in Nora's ear, making her giggle.

"So do I," Nora responded as she turned his way and received his soft, lingering kisses.

Making out with him was a favorite delight she never got enough of. Rodney slipped his fingers inside her blouse to caress the breast Eddie was not using, and Nora inhaled involuntarily.

"You're gonna get it now," Nora threatened with false anger.

"Oh, no!" Rodney exclaimed, looking up, clasping his forehead in feigned dread.

"You better hide where I can't find you," Nora recommended sternly.

Rodney shot up off the couch and Nora heard the bedroom door close; her groin felt warm as she thought about what she was going to do to him. Doctors recommended six weeks before Rodney could penetrate her so she was basically helping him masturbate at this point. She loved doing it though; it made him so happy.

On their wedding night, Rodney led Nora in a discussion about his understanding of sex and the Bible's many references. He was most interested in what she was expecting and, taking his lead, she became interested in what he wanted. Together they asked God to lead and guide them, then they decided on what they wanted to do and what both of them were comfortable doing.

When Nora opened the bedroom door, Rodney lay spread eagle on the bed, unclothed, except for a giant grin.

"I found you!" Nora laughed, as she laid Eddie in the bassinet and walked to the end of the bed.

"Be gentle," Rodney groaned dramatically, then whimpered with exaggerated sob. "It's my first time."

"Liar," Nora mumbled as she began to stroke Rodney's already swollen organ.

Rodney moaned and sighed blissfully as Nora's actions sent waves of ecstasy through Rodney's body. When the sexual tension released, she crawled up to lay beside him.

"I'm bursting with love for you," Rodney whispered, as he gently rubbed her entire body. "I thought I loved you before our wedding night; but it is nothing compared to my love for you now. God knew what he was doing when he led me to you."

"Imagine six weeks from now," Nora cooed, snuggling close to him, "when I can feel you inside me."

"Ohhh, I am imagining, Dear One," Rodney interrupted. "I can't help but imagine it."

After fantasizing for a while about that special night, they rose to fix dinner; Nora changed Eddie's diaper and wrapped him in a chest carrier. Nora discovered that any task she did with Rodney, with God's blessing on their marriage, was a pleasure. They had learned, in their seven short months together, to share everything.

Rodney, as a result of his friendship with Howard, now had an office position with the football organization in addition to being the unofficial team chaplain. It's not hard to imagine the stresses and temptations of a national football team member, and the millions of dollars they made increased that stress in some players rather than reducing it. Rodney's goal was to keep them focused on God and Jesus through Bible study and prayer. Nora's conversations with Rodney made her realize that the 'sinner's prayer' she prayed in church so long ago was only the beginning of her journey with Jesus. With Rodney's help, she learned what the Bible said and she took everything to Jesus in prayer. Looking back on her life, she concluded, if she had been following Jesus earnestly when she met Howard, she would never have gone to Catherine's house at any time which would have prevented the rape. She thanked God daily for making a provision for her ignorance and bringing Rodney into her life.

It turns out that Rodney, who was five years older than Nora, had never intended to go to any college, let alone the Christian college in Nora's town. Though his grandfather was a devout Christian, Rodney's family participated in every kind of activity except church. Both of his foul-mouthed, alcoholic, violent parents loved hard rock and heavy metal along with R and X rated movies. In their opinion, they were raising their son to be free of all the Christian restrictions promoted by his grandfather or any other Christian. In exercising this freedom, Rodney experimented with the drugs available at concerts and porn establishments. One night, in a drug-induced trance, some beautiful, non-human creatures met him, and offered him ecstasy he would never forget. When he accepted their offer, they led him into an ethereal place void of light where darkness was palatable. After a while, his legs crumbled beneath him having lost strength. Though he felt acute sexual sensations he had never felt before, he was keenly aware that life was being drained from his blood as though a vampire was sucking on his neck.

"Don't be afraid," one of the creatures whispered as he lay on top of Rodney's limp body. "Let yourself go and bask in ecstasy for eternity."

"Jesus saves," Rodney heard his grandfather declare from afar. "Jesus saves."

"Ecstasy," the creature hissed slowly as something like lightening shot through Rodney's body making a long, loud howl escape from Rodney's soul.

Rodney's choice was crystal clear: follow the creature and die or follow Jesus and live.

"I'll. Follow," Rodney rasped as he had to force out the words, "Jesus."

Rodney then woke in an alley next to a concert hall with the sun breaking through the blackness of night. His pants were undone and his zipper unzipped; his cell phone and wallet gone. Struggling to stand up, he stumbled toward the sun, and asked the first policeman he saw to call his grandfather. His grandfather, Ned, picked him up and, after Rodney shared the experience, Ned thanked God with tears for saving his grandson. Rodney moved in with Ned and began learning that God, as creator[16], expects to be obeyed,[17] and that Jesus became God in the flesh[18] to die for Adam's disobedience[19], so that we, God's children, could be reconciled to God,[20] and live with him for eternity[21]. Vowing to follow Jesus the rest of his life, Rodney, with his grandfather's help, got enrolled in Bible college, thinking he would eventually pastor a church, and, never in a million years, did he picture himself working for a national football league and befriending football heroes and legends.

At the dinner table, Nora asked Rodney about Howard's reaction to Catherine's nude photos.

"He's probably devastated," Rodney guessed. "He's been sharing her with a few men occasionally; now he's sharing her with the world. She loves the attention; she loves showing off; I think she's foolish enough to make porn a career."

"But, he could use this situation to tell the world how wrong she is," Nora offered. "Media attention will be on him now, right?"

With a mouth full of food, Rodney stopped chewing and stared at her.

"Datz r...," he finished chewing and swallowed quickly. "That's right. That's right. I'm going to tell him that. You are a precious gift from God, Nora."

At the office the next day, Rodney greeted Howard enthusiastically.

"What's up?" Howard asked with a sigh.

"Nora made a brilliant statement last night," Rodney began. "She is seeing your situation as an opportunity to tell the world how wrong Catherine is."

To Rodney's surprise, Howard stoic face broke into a grin.

"You won't be surprised to hear this," Howard responded. "I'm seeing the same thing, and I was hoping God would send me confirmation. You both are amazing!"

"God is amazing!" Rodney blurted and Howard laughed as he nodded in agreement.

"I've already received a hundred requests for interviews," Howard added. "When you called, I was on my way to the press office. Want to come with me?"

The two men, physical opposites: short and lean versus tall and muscular, walked down the hall to the press office. When they emerged, Howard's first interview was scheduled.

"I want you to record this," Howard requested to Rodney. "I don't trust the media. They'll report what they want to report; I want all of it reported."

When the news van arrived, they decided to interview on the football field. The team's press office made sure Howard looked good for the camera. Some team members, who were fellow Christians, showed up with cell phones ready to record. Rodney stood by the cameraman with a camera; unknown to Howard, Rodney had arranged for a live broadcast on multiple social media outlets. The producer situated Howard so sunlight would hit him properly as well as the news personality, who was clutching a microphone. The producer called for a take.

"This is Morgan Dopler at the Rounder Stadium with Howard Shay, lead quarter back for the Rounders," Morgan began. "Thank you for taking time for News33, Howard."

Morgan tilted the microphone to Howard so he could be heard.

"Thank you for having me," Howard responded politely with a smile.

Morgan tilted the microphone to himself.

"It's been reported that your wife, Catherine, has signed a multi-million dollar contract for a spread in "All Things for All Men"," Morgan continued and, with a smile added, "It is anticipated that she will bear 'all things.'"

Morgan tilted the microphone to Howard.

"Right," Howard agreed looking straight into the camera. "She informed me this morning that she had made that decision."

Morgan tilted the microphone to himself.

"An honor for her, I would think?" Morgan guessed. "Not many women have been honored in such a way."

Morgan tilted the microphone to Howard.

"In the secular world, yes, it is considered an honor; a great honor," Howard agreed, "but..."

Morgan tilted the microphone to himself.

"The secular world?" Morgan questioned.

The producer yelled 'cut!' but Howard grabbed the microphone and, when Morgan reached for it, Howard held him at arm's length.

"In God's world, this is wrong," Howard stated.

The producer stepped in front of Howard and a team member tackled him then held him down. Rodney stepped back to get a shot of the producer who was thrashing and cussing.

"The news camera is off," Howard observed. "Can you get it back on?"

A team member yanked the camera from the cameraman as another team member pulled the cameraman away. The cameraman thrust his elbow into the team member's stomach, breaking free, trying to retrieve the camera. The team member caught him, pulled him down, and struggled to keep him down. Rodney recorded it.

"It's rolling," said the team member holding the camera.

"In God's world, what my wife is doing is wrong," Howard continued. "Nudity is private. Nudity is a gift God has given to a husband and a wife; no-one else.[22]"

Multiple police sirens were getting closer.

"God designed sex to be performed in private by a husband and wife to make a family,[23]" Howard added.

Police cars entered the stadium, and Howard let go of Morgan, handing him the microphone. The producer was helped up; the cameraman was released and he was given the camera which was still recording as well as Rodney, who took a few steps away from police to get them in the shot.

"What's the problem?" one of the officers asked.

No-one answered.

"We got a hundred or so 911 calls that there was a problem here," the officer continued, studying everyone.

No-one responded.

"Is anyone hurt?" the officer tried again. "Is anyone pressing charges?"

"I'm sorry for the inconvenience," Howard finally offered. "I think it's a false alarm."

The officer looked at his comrades and, when they had nothing to add, they drove off the field.

"I'm sorry," Howard said to the producer.

"Are you kidding me?" the producer exclaimed. "I can't wait to air this! You just secured our number one spot in tonight's ratings. Listen, I'll arrange a serious interview, OK? Would you be willing to debate this?"

"It would be my extreme pleasure," Howard assured him, offering his hand to shake, which the producer took.

When Howard entered the football office, the first person he met said the owner, Roger Boggs, was holding on the phone for him. Howard went to his office and took the call.

"What! The! Hell!" Roger roared. "My field ain't no place for one of your religious rants! I'm fining you for breaking the rules - one million dollars!"

The coach burst through Howard's office door. Howard put the call on speaker.

"Yes, Sir," Howard answered calmly as he was smiling while Roger ranted. "I understand, Sir."

"You better understand, Dumbass!" Roger bellowed. "This club don't need no religious zealots."

Howard said nothing and Roger ended the call.

"How much?" the coach asked.

"One! Million!" Howard answered with a chuckle.

"He's not really mad, then," the coach concluded. "He's appeasing someone."

"I agree," Howard responded and he stood up.

Both men left the office to attend a team meeting.

"That video already has a million views," someone yelled at them.

"You better win this next game," the coach threatened.

"This is way more important than football," Howard replied confidently.

Chapter 5

After Catherine finished the photoshoot, she sent happy texts to Nora, and posted party pictures of herself and the Beautiful Rich. Her followers were now over a million. Then one night, Anna, the nanny, called Nora saying there was an intruder and Howard was hurt. Adding Rodney to the call, he asked Anna for more information then he decided to drive to Howard's.

"Do you want to go?" Rodney asked Nora, seeing her ashen face.

"I think I should," Nora murmured, and she packed Eddie in the carrier.

As they approached the house, twenty or so police cars and two squads were parked on the lawn. Medics were pulling stretchers out of the squad. Police would not let them pass so Rodney called Anna; she came out to get them. Inside, debris covered the floor from a broken vase. Anna led them to the living room where Nora gasped and turned away from a knife, surrounded by a circle of blood, protruding from Howard's stomach; another man was laying close by, unconscious, but no wounds were apparent. Anna took Eddie in the carrier. Catherine was on the couch, staring lifelessly at the scene. When she saw Nora, she reached for her. Rodney knelt beside Howard, praying.

"He's a stalker," Catherine whispered, trembling as she pointed to the unconscious man. "I don't know how he got in. Electronic security is everywhere."

"What happened?" Nora asked.

"I was done working out and walked to the fridge in the kitchen. The stalker grabbed me from behind, lifting me up like he thought he was going to carry me somewhere," Catherine recounted. "I kicked the fridge which pushed him off balance and he fell, but he grabbed my ankle as I tried to run. I screamed for Howard. The man jumped up and pulled a knife, watching for Howard, so I was able to get a few feet away from him and call 911."

As medics put the man on a stretcher, he groaned in pain.

"I think he has broken bones," Catherine guessed then she continued. "The man had the knife pointed at Howard and Howard backed away from him toward the living room. As they passed me, I smashed a vase on the man's back then he turned toward me. Howard bounded at him grabbing his throat. I could hear the sirens so I opened the door. When I looked back, they were in the living room and Howard was on the floor with a knife in his stomach. The man was laying close by, unconscious."

Medics put Howard on a stretcher and wheeled him out. Rodney followed, glancing at Nora. Catherine continued.

"When I rushed to Howard, he looked at me so tenderly and touched my cheek," Catherine moaned then she stared at Nora. "There's a knife in his stomach and he..."

She broke down in sobs and Nora pulled her close. The medic asked if Catherine was coming and Nora said she would drive her. They heard the sirens as the squads raced to the hospital.

"Don't you know how much he loves you?" Nora questioned, astounded that Catherine didn't seem to know. "Even though you put him through hell, he stands by you."

Her sobs increased, shaking her entire body.

"I see it," she finally whimpered. "I see what I've done[24]."

"What do you see?" Nora asked softly.

"I see the hundreds of times and ways I hurt him," Catherine confessed as she stared at nothing. "I see how I hated my babies."

Catherine turned to study Nora's face.

"I see how I tortured you," Catherine whispered as tears streamed.

"Do you want to change?" Nora offered softly. "Do you think you can follow Jesus now?"

"I do want to change," Catherine announced, as though she was surprised at her own words. "I can follow Jesus now, Nora. I want to tell Howard!"

Catherine got into Nora and Rodney's car, and they rushed to the hospital. Howard was in surgery when they arrived, and Catherine was led to a room to sign papers. Then a nurse led the three of them to a waiting area. In a couple of hours, a nurse notified Catherine that the knife was removed and Howard was in Recovery; all his vital signs looked good. It was close to dawn when they were allowed to see Howard, and then it was through a glass. Catherine wept like Nora had never seen her weep, and she clung to the window. Though Howard was strapped tightly, he turned his head toward her as much as he could and lifted his thumb as high as he could. The three of them laughed and then Catherine started to sing; Nora and Howard put their arms behind her back and sang with her:

"Jesus loves me, this I know,

For the Bible tells me so,

Little ones to him belong,

We are weak; but he is strong.[25]"

As they sang the chorus, "Yes, Jesus loves me," a nurse made them leave. Catherine blew on the window making steam with her breath and drew a heart, throwing him kisses as she backed away from him. When Catherine was allowed to visit Howard in the hospital, he was sitting up when she entered the room and his face lit up at the sight of her. Putting her arm behind his neck and the other across his chest, she kissed his cheek. He turned his head to touch her lips; then he lifted her onto his lap like she weighed nothing. She stroked his hair and studied his face. He stayed quiet thinking she had something to say.

"I'm following Jesus," Catherine finally whispered simply.

Howard's face puckered with tears as he looked to Heaven and raised his arms straight up.

"Thank you, Lord!" Howard yelled, and he didn't care who heard him.

"Amen," a few people responded in adjoining rooms.

Then he pulled Catherine as close as possible without crushing her. As God's presence fell on them, they both sobbed with joy.

"This is the happiest day of my life!" Howard exclaimed, stroking her hair.

"I feel like a new person," Catherine mused. "It feels like something in me came alive."

"You are a new person," Howard agreed. "I'll show you in the Bible[26]."

"I'm sorry it took a knife in your stomach…," Catherine started.

"A small price," Howard interrupted, shaking his head. "No, it's not a price; it was a gift. That knife was the gift of your salvation."

Howard moved over so that Catherine could lay beside him but they were interrupted in a few minutes when a nurse came in to take vitals. Though Catherine moved to a chair, they could not stop looking at each other. The nurse left.

"I better go," Catherine stated sadly then whispered as she bent close to him. "I want to strip you and have my way with you."

"Ooohhhh, pleeeeease," Howard begged, reaching for her but she backed away; he begged again, "One little kiss?"

Catherine touched his lips then stepped away as his hands started creeping under her shirt.

"Do you have doctor's permission for that activity, Sir?" Catherine teased.

"I'm going to get his permission next time I see him," Howard exclaimed. "Count on that!"

Catherine backed away from him, throwing kisses. He looked like he was going to die as he watched her depart.

A week after Howard's release, he and Catherine were seated on a News33 TV set getting prepped for an interview about the nude photoshoot. It had published, selling thousands of copies; their phones and computers were bursting with calls and emails ranging from offers for future shoots to death threats. With Rodney's help, Catherine and

Howard agreed on what the Bible said about nudity and on what would be done with the money from the shoot.

The producer, Michael Fairchild, greeted them along with Morgan Dopler. As Michael had predicted, the interview on the football field got the highest ratings of the night and year-to-date; he was hoping for a similar outcome tonight.

"Morgan," Howard greeted extending his hand, and Morgan took it.

"We've got Security here," Morgan quipped, "so don't grab the mic."

"It's all yours," Howard laughed.

Another newswoman, a veteran of twenty-some years, Monica Auburn, walked onto the set and everyone was introduced. Technicians followed to attach microphones, test lighting and check make-up.

"Is everyone comfortable?" Michael asked. "I'm going to start counting from five."

He paused for a moment, studying the group.

"Five, four, three, two, one," Michael counted then said, "Roll it."

"This is Morgan Dopler for News33," Morgan began, "with my co-anchor, Monica Auburn, and guests, Howard Shay, lead quarterback for the Rounders, and his wife, Catherine, whose impressive spread in "All Things for All Men" just hit the stands."

"How was the shoot, Catherine?" Morgan asked.

"It was fun," Catherine answered honestly, with some flush in her cheeks. "They do everything possible to make you comfortable and happy...like your producer did here tonight."

"I can't imagine what it would be like to 'bare all things', if I may," Monica chuckled, "in front of camera and crew...especially with those two gorgeous, naked men."

"Aaahhmm," Catherine paused to think, "it's not like a party. You're listening to directions and, with the lights, you can't see anyone."

"Weren't the men touching you?" Monica pressed.

"Sometimes," Catherine answered casually, "but it was a light touch, meant to suggest. I wasn't concentrating on that. The goal was to give the producer and photographer what they wanted."

"What did they want, exactly?" Monica continued.

"I believe they wanted 'art', like Michelangelo maybe," Catherine answered. "They are capturing the idea or the concept of sexual arousal."

"Howard," Morgan jumped in, "we heard your views last week on public nudity, which appear to be opposite to your wife's."

"That is how it appears, but, we experienced a miracle last week, didn't we, Catherine?" Howard prompted.

"We did," Catherine agreed, nodding, and continued before anyone could interrupt. "I was born again[27] last week. I have turned away from public nudity and anything else Jesus is against."

"Did this spread hurt anyone, Howard?" Monica pressed, wanting to change the subject. "I mean, Catherine says it's art. She's getting money for it, lot's of money."

"Catherine is donating the money to help mothers in need," Howard began, "and I could give you many reasons for keeping nudity private, but the most important reason is God. God created nudity for a husband and wife to enjoy in their own garden. It's not meant to be shared or photographed or recorded."

"You have two children," Monica stated to Catherine, quickly changing the subject again.

"Yes," Catherine answered uncomfortably, looking at Howard.

"One lives with you?" Monica continued. "The other..."

"Lives with his father," Catherine finished.

"And, Howard, you have a son," Monica stated.

"Not yet," Howard answered then he turned to Catherine with a smile, "but we hope to."

"Our sources say that Nora Phillips gave birth to your son," Monica stated flatly.

"She did give birth to a son, but not my son," Howard insisted with confidence.

Monica held up a sheet of paper.

"I've got paperwork right here stating you are the father," Monica cooed.

Howard looked at Catherine who looked back at him with horror.

"What's wrong?" Howard asked, leaning toward her with apprehension; then Catherine stood with her back to the camera and leaned close to Howard's ear.

"You are the father," Catherine whispered.

Howard studied her face.

"How can you call yourself 'Christian' amidst this adulterous behavior?" Monica challenged with excitement.

"Cut!" yelled Michael, the producer.

"No!" yelled Monica.

Howard rose and looked directly at Monica.

"We are sinners!" Howard exclaimed. "We make mistakes. We call ourselves Christians because we turn from those mistakes and strive to please God. Then God forgives[28] us because of the sacrifice Jesus made on the cross[29]."

Howard gently led Catherine a few steps away from the group then he paused, waiting for Catherine to explain. Michael, the producer, followed and ripped off the microphones.

"I didn't know it was an ambush," Michael declared as he turned to face a furious, cussing Monica.

"In Beverly Hills," Catherine said softly. "I found you in Nora's room, asleep, with your pants down. I assumed you had sex with her, so I took the bed covers. When Eddie was born, I bribed some people to have a DNA test done. I was just waiting for the opportunity to accuse you and Nora."

Catherine laid her head on Howard's chest as loud, deep sobs escaped from her soul. Howard lifted her into his arms to get her away from the

TV crew, and put her in the passenger seat of their car; he knelt beside her.

"Did she say I had sex with her?" Howard repeated with disbelief.

"After Beverly Hills, I never talked to her until you were attacked," Catherine whimpered, "then her only concern was me and you. But Howard…"

Catherine laid her hands on his massive shoulders.

"A pair of panties were in the bed clothes," Catherine continued. "Nora's DNA…"

Howard's phone rang.

"It's Rodney," Howard informed Catherine as he stepped away from the car, then he said, "Hey, Bro."

"Hey," Rodney replied softly. "Your interview is on social media. Are you OK? Is Catherine OK?"

"Well, aaahhh," Howard responded then let out an embarrassed chuckle. "I got to ask you, did I have sex with Nora?"

"Did you get drunk in Beverly Hills?" Rodney countered.

"Afraid so," Howard admitted, shaking his head. "I did get stinkin' drunk. First mistake, I guess."

"Right," Rodney answered. "Nora said you thought she was Catherine."

"Is…is Nora OK with this?" Howard began but Rodney interrupted.

"She calls it rape," Rodney declared bluntly. "She was going to abort the baby but God led me to her."

Rodney recounted how God had led Rodney to the abortion center.

"Why didn't you tell me?" Howard cried in anguish then he walked back to Catherine, knelt beside her and looked into her eyes with pleading. "Why didn't somebody tell me?"

"It's between you, Nora and God, isn't it?" Rodney answered. "You three have to work it out."

"God, I'm sorry," Howard whispered as he looked to Heaven then added. "Thank you for taking care of Nora and the baby."

"That's a perfect start. But let me assure you," Rodney continued, "Nora is happy now; we're happy now."

"What a mess!" Howard exclaimed as he thought about the complications of sharing his son with the innocent woman he had violated and the man she married.

"Yes, sin makes a mess, to be sure," Rodney agreed. "But if we give the situation to God, he not only cleans it up, he improves it."

"We got a lot to talk about," Howard offered, looking up at Catherine. "Tomorrow?"

Catherine nodded, pulling him as close to her as she could.

"Tomorrow," Rodney agreed and ended the call.

Howard rested against Catherine as she gently rubbed his back and stroked his hair.

"God will make it alright," Catherine finally offered. "I was a mess..."

Howard pushed himself up to study her perfect face; a face now radiant because of the new life God had breathed into her[30].

"And look at you now," Howard interrupted as his own face brightened, like it always did when he looked at her, then he requested softly, "Tell me again you're following Jesus."

"I'm following Jesus," Catherine repeated with a shy smile.

"Yeah, God will make it alright," Howard concluded. "Want to go home?"

Catherine nodded then Howard closed the car door.

"It's your turn to peel potatoes," Howard announced through the closed window.

"Oh! No!" Catherine protested as he rushed to the driver's side of the car.

As he got in the car, she turned to make her argument that it was his turn. He was laughing hysterically as they drove off the parking lot.

Isaiah 41:10 KJV

"So do not fear, for I am with you; do not be dismayed, for I am your God. I will strengthen you and help you; I will uphold you with my righteous right hand."

Dear Reader: God's 'righteous right hand' is Jesus. Jesus will lead you away from behavior and situations that hurt, damage and destroy. Follow him by reading the Bible and praying. The New King James Version is the best Bible to start with. God be with you.

[1] Romans 10:17 KJV "So then faith cometh by hearing, and hearing by the word of God."

[2] Virginity is very important to God as demonstrated in Deuteronomy 22:13-21. In these verses, God commands a woman to be stoned to death if she engaged in sex before marriage.

[3] Jesus turned water into wine, John chapter 2.

[4] In John chapter 3, Jesus instructs Nicodemus on the importance of being 'born again'.

[5] Hebrews 13:20-21 KJV "Now the God of peace..."Make you perfect in every good work to do his will, working in you that which is wellpleasing in his sight, through Jesus Christ..."

[6] 1 John 2:2 KJV "He (Jesus) is the propitiation (payment) for our sins, and not for ours only but also for the sins of the whole world."

[7] John 16:13 KJV "Howbeit when he, the Spirit of truth, is come, he will guide you into all truth..."

[8] 2 Corinthians 6:14 KJV "Be ye not unequally yoked together with unbelievers..."

[9] John 10:10 KJV

[10] 2 Corinthians 6:14 KJV "14 Be ye not unequally yoked together with unbelievers: for what fellowship hath righteousness with unrighteousness? and what communion hath light with darkness?"

[11] Acts 8:29 KJV "Then the Spirit said unto Philip, Go near, and join thyself to this chariot."

[12] Ephesians 5:25 KJV "Husbands, love your wives, even as Christ also loved the church, and gave himself for it..."

[13] 2 Corinthians 6:14 KJV "Be ye not unequally yoked together with unbelievers: for what fellowship hath righteousness with unrighteousness? and what communion hath light with darkness?"

[14] 1 Corinthians 13:4-8 KJV "4 Charity (love) suffereth long, and is kind; charity envieth not; charity vaunteth not it self, is not puffed up, 5 Doth not behave itself unseemly, seeketh not her own, is not easily provoked, thinketh no evil; 6 Rejoiceth not in iniquity, but rejoiceth in the truth; 7 Beareth all things, believeth all things, hopeth all things, endureth all things. 8 Charity never faileth:

[15] Exodus 20:17 KJV "Thou shalt not covet thy neighbour's house, thou shalt not covet thy neighbour's wife, nor his manservant, nor his maidservant, nor his ox, nor his ass, nor any thing that is thy neighbour's."

[16] Isaiah 45:12 KJV "...I have made the earth, and created man upon it: I...have stretched out the heavens..."

[17] John 14:21 KJV "He that hath my commandments, and keepeth them, he it is that loveth me: and he that loveth me shall be loved of my Father, and I will love him, and will manifest myself to him."

[18] John 1:14 KJV "And the Word (Jesus) was made flesh, and dwelt among us..."

[19] Genesis 2:17 KJV God speaking, "But of the tree of the knowledge of good and evil, thou (Adam) shalt not eat of it: for in the day that thou eatest thereof thou shalt surely die."

[20] Colossians 1:14 KJV "In whom (Jesus) we have redemption through his blood, even the forgiveness of sins..."

[21] Psalm 23:6 KJV "Surely goodness and mercy shall follow me all the days of my life: and I will dwell in the house of the Lord for ever."

[22] Matthew 5:28 KJV "But I (Jesus) say unto you, That whosoever looketh on a woman to lust after her hath committed adultery with her already in his heart."

[23] 1 Corinthians 7:2 KJV "Nevertheless, to avoid fornication, let every man have his own wife, and let every woman have her own husband."

[24] 2 Corinthians 4:3-4 KJV "3 But if our gospel be hid, it is hid to them that are lost: 4 In whom the god of this world hath blinded the minds of them which believe not..."

[25] "Jesus Loves Me" by Anna Bartlett Warner, 1859

[26] 2 Corinthians 5:17 KJV "Therefore if any man be in Christ, he is a new creature: old things are passed away; behold, all things are become new."

[27] John 3:5 KJV "Jesus answered, Verily, verily, I say unto thee, Except a man be born of water and of the Spirit, he cannot enter into the kingdom of God."

[28] 1 John 1:9 KJV "If we confess our sins, he is faithful and just to forgive us our sins, and to cleanse us from all unrighteousness."

[29] 1 Peter 2:24 KJV "Who his (Jesus) own self bare our sins in his own body on the tree, that we, being dead to sins, should live unto righteousness:"

[30] Genesis 2:7 KJV "And the Lord God formed man of the dust of the ground, and breathed into his nostrils the breath of life; and man became a living soul."

* 9 7 9 8 2 2 3 8 0 9 5 8 6 *